The Queen & Mr Brown
A Night in the Natural History Museum

James Francis Wilkins

Published by the Natural History Museum, London

For my parents

Once again many thanks to
Steve Woods and Colin Ziegler
for their advice and support

First published by the Natural History Museum
Cromwell Road, London SW7 5BD
© Natural History Museum, London, 2016
Text and illustrations © James Francis Wilkins

ISBN 978 0 565 09376 1

A catalogue record for this book is available from the
British Library.

Reproduction by Saxon Digital Services
Printed in China by C&C Offset Printing Co., Ltd

The Queen worked hard. She had always worked
hard and carried out her duties as best she could.
Everyone loved and respected her and she enjoyed
the life she had been given. But she did sometimes
wish she could have one more life, one for her
secret passion.

Even as a little girl the Queen had been
fascinated by nature. She loved to spend her
days climbing trees, paddling in ponds and
looking under stones to see what was there.

And when she grew up and had some free
time she would escape with Mr Brown to
a wild place and observe nature.

She wanted to understand nature's mysteries: the migration of butterflies and the music of whales, why there were no dinosaurs any more and why there were fewer and fewer bees. Sometimes this passion of hers was difficult to control.

At a royal garden party she saw a spotted flycatcher perched in a tree. She wanted to shout out,
'LOOK A SPOTTED FLYCATCHER AT THIS TIME OF YEAR IN CENTRAL LONDON! HOW AMAZING!'

Luckily she managed to control herself and kept quiet.

But that evening she did what she had been meaning to do for ages. She wrote to the Director of the Natural History Museum.

Dear Director,

I have had the privilege and pleasure of visiting your Museum on several occasions. As you may know I have a deep interest in nature but very little time to pursue it. Therefore I want to ask a very special favour of you.

Could I possibly visit your Museum after hours, when all the visitors have left, so I can study everything undisturbed and at length? I promise to leave everything exactly as I find it. If you can grant me this wish I will be eternally grateful.

With kind regards,

Your Queen

PS. And can I bring along my friend Mr Brown?

The very next day she received a reply. 'Your Majesty, I would be delighted to grant your request! Just let me know when you are coming and I will arrange everything.'

And so it was that late one evening the Queen and Mr Brown came to be standing at the entrance to the Museum. They were greeted with open arms by the Director who gave them a key and asked just one thing. 'Please lock the door behind you when you leave.'

The entrance hall seemed enormous with no-one
in it. 'So Mr Brown, where shall we begin? We
have the whole Museum to ourselves!'

'I fancy visiting the woolly mammoths. I always think they look like elephants in fur coats. Sadly there are none alive today.'

They walked down deserted corridors, crossed cavernous halls and finally found the mammoths. 'Here we are Mr Brown. Isn't he gorgeous! But shall we have a snack before I start reading about him?'

They sat on a nearby bench and the Queen
got out some biscuits. 'Look what I've brought
Mr Brown, gingersnaps – your favourites!
Please try not to leave any crumbs. We want
to make a good impression!'

The Queen began to read and Mr Brown stretched out
next to her and closed his eyes. When she had finished
looking at the first case she moved on to the next and
then the one after. Mr Brown followed. 'It's going to be
a long night', he thought.

Suddenly Mr Brown pricked up his ears. He had heard something odd. He looked around but there was nothing there. He looked again and thought he saw faces staring at him. He pressed himself hard against the Queen's legs. 'What is it Mr Brown, are you feeling lonely?'

Just after she said this there was a deafening
clatter of wings and a big black bird with a
huge yellow bill swooped into the room.

'Do I smell gingersnaps?' he asked. The Queen had experienced many strange things in her life and she kept her cool. 'Well, yes actually…would you care for one?'

'Thanks very much – I don't mind if I do!' the bird replied, and he hopped down next to them. The Queen offered the bird, which she recognised as a toucan, a gingersnap. He broke off a piece with his bill, tilted his head up and swallowed it. Then he turned his head and squawked…

...'IT'S ALRIGHT!
YOU CAN COME OUT NOW.
THEY'RE FRIENDLY!'

Mr Brown knew now what he had heard. Faces peered
in through the entrance and Mr Brown felt himself
trembling as strange animals rushed towards them.

Ptarmigan, toad, penguin, bat,

albatross, anteater, rhinoceros, rat.

They streamed in without end...

...and surrounded the Queen and Mr Brown. 'Leave some space! Leave some space!' the toucan cried. 'We don't want to scare our guests.' The toucan turned to the Queen. 'So what brings you here at this time of night – we normally have the place to ourselves?'

'We're just here to find out about all the wonderful animals that live on Earth.' the Queen replied innocently. 'Well, you've come to the right place,' said the toucan, 'and we really are wonderful. Would you like to learn some more?'

The toucan whispered something to his friend the polar bear. 'Yes, yes, good idea,' the bear replied, 'Just leave it to me.' She rose up on her back legs and roared 'Q-U-I-E-T' and miraculously the chattering stopped. 'My friends, we have special guests who would like to meet us. Please line up in a row so we can be introduced and explain what makes each of us special.'

The animals jostled around to form a line, pushing and shoving each other until they had all found a place. Then the toucan started introducing them.

It was all so familiar to the Queen, just like being
at one of her garden parties at the Palace. With her
good manners she found a kind word for everyone.

The toucan introduced an albatross. 'I can fly for 10,000 miles without touching down' he said. The Queen was impressed. 'How do you do it?' 'It's simple really,' replied the albatross, 'We have the best technology. We've been working on it for 30 million years.' 'That is a long time', said the Queen admiringly.

Next was a hedgehog with a distinctive country accent.
'When the weathur gets cold Oi finds a nice cosy place
fur meself, makes a nest of leaves n' grass n' things
and then Oi curls up in a ball and sleeps for the rest
of wintur. It's me way of saving energy.'
'How very sensible of you', said the Queen.

And so it went on and every animal had a special ability,
even the smallest of them. The toucan listened to a tiny
flea: 'He says he can jump 150 times his own height!'

'How wonderful!' cried the Queen. 'If I could do that
I could jump over the Palace.' The animals chortled.
They were warming to her.

Then came a silkmoth. 'I can smell…'
he began in a teeny-weeny voice, 'I can
smell my wife six miles away!'

'Oooh! The very thought!' the Queen
exclaimed and she looked quite shocked,
much to the amusement of the animals.

A bat squeaked 'I can catch insects in the dark!' This
gave the Queen an idea. Midges often buzzed above
her bed in the summer, keeping her awake, and so she
invited the bat to stay at her summer home in Scotland.

When the animals heard this they clapped and cheered.
Loudest of all was a purple frog who jumped up and
down shouting 'Bravo!' The Queen bent close to him.
'And what's your speciality I would like to know?'

The frog stopped moving and suddenly...THWAPP!!
He zapped her on the tip of her nose.

'I can catch...I can catch...' he croaked between
giggles, 'I can catch flies with my TONGUE!' he
said, before falling over backwards laughing.

The polar bear turned to Mr Brown. 'Now it's your turn to show us what you can do. We'd love to know about it.'

Mr Brown froze. He was horrified. 'I c…c…can't do anything clever', he thought.

But then, as sometimes happens when everything seems hopeless, he had an idea. He stood a long time without moving and, when no-one was expecting it…

The animals erupted and those with feet stamped them on the floor. Mr Brown looked around at the beaming faces. Did they really think that was clever? A tortoise called out 'I'd love to do that but I know if I tried I'd get stuck on my back.'

The Queen was thinking frantically. If the polar bear should ask her the same question what would she do? Sure enough the bear turned to her and said 'What your friend did was truly remarkable. We'd love to know what you can do!'

The Queen smiled sweetly, raised
both of her arms and...

...spun around on one leg.

'I CAN DO A PIROUETTE!' she said.

'Beautiful…simply beautiful!' the bear bellowed
and there were cries of 'What style!' 'What elegance!'
'What grace!' A millipede called out 'I've always
dreamt of doing that but I know I never will.'

There was general pandemonium and the animals
forgot about standing in line. They chatted excitedly
with one another, exchanging the latest animal gossip.

The Queen suddenly had a thought.

'The time Mr Brown! We must go. There's
work to do. I have to open Parliament today.'

She spoke to the polar bear and told her they
had to go. 'Oh what a pity, the party is just
beginning!' the bear said. 'You must come
again as soon as you can and next time we'll
lay on something special.'

The Queen said they would love to come again and turned to wave goodbye to all the animals. There were cries of 'Good-bye! Good-bye! It was so nice to get to know you.' 'The pleasure was entirely ours.' the Queen replied as she and Mr Brown headed for the exit.

The Queen locked the Museum door as the Director had requested and the two friends walked down the steps into Brompton Road and hurried back to the Palace.

The sky was pink with the dawn and they passed a few early
risers, but they hardly noticed anything. They were still
thinking about their extraordinary night in the Museum.

'Well Mr Brown..that really was something. Who would have believed all of the amazing things they can do, and they were all so friendly. Aren't our fellow animals wonderful!'

Mr Brown wasn't listening. He was just so proud that they had liked his trick and was busy thinking up a new one to impress them with next time.